When I Feel Good about Myself

WRITTEN BY Cornelia Maude Spelman

ILLUSTRATED BY Kathy Parkinson

Albert Whitman & Company
Chicago, Illinois

For Anthony—just as he is.—C.M.S.

For Brianna, with lots of love.—K.P.

Books by Cornelia Maude Spelman

After Charlotte's Mom Died ~ *Mama and Daddy Bear's Divorce*
Your Body Belongs to You

The Way I Feel Books:

When I Care about Others ~ *When I Feel Angry*
When I Feel Good about Myself ~ *When I Feel Jealous* ~ *When I Feel Worried*
When I Feel Sad ~ *When I Feel Scared* ~ *When I Miss You*

Library of Congress Cataloging-in-Publication Data

Spelman, Cornelia.
When I feel good about myself / by Cornelia Maude Spelman ;
illustrated by Kathy Parkinson.
p. cm. — (The way I feel)
Summary: A young guinea pig explains that self-confidence comes from learning
new things without being afraid of making mistakes and to remember
that everyone has different qualities that make them lovable.
[1. Self-confidence — Fiction. 2. Individuality — Fiction. 3. Guinea pigs — Fiction.]
I. Parkinson, Kathy, ill. II. Title. III. Series.
PZ7.S74727Whe 2003 [E] — dc21 2002011324

Published in 2003 by Albert Whitman & Company
ISBN 13: 978-0-8075-8887-1 (hardcover)
ISBN 13: 978-0-8075-8901-4 (paperback)

Printed in China
18 17 16 15 14 13 LP 20 19 18 17 16 15

Design by Carol Gildar

For more information about Albert Whitman & Company,
please visit our web site at www.albertwhitman.com.
Please visit Cornelia at her web site: www.corneliaspelman.com.

Note to Parents and Teachers

Children feel good about themselves—develop self-esteem—when their parents and other important adults show regard for their inherent value ("Somebody loves me just as I am").

They feel good about themselves when their interaction with their world is successful and acknowledged by those around them. As they grow and learn—to dress themselves, to build with blocks, to make a painting, to throw and catch a ball, to help others, to make friends—their success gives them the confidence to try new tasks ("I like learning new things").

Each child is unique. We need to help our children see that it's good that we are all different. We don't have to look like others or have the same skills or interests ("When I paint or make things, they are not like anyone else's").

While it's nice to have a special talent, those children who don't have one need to know that they are just as valuable as those who do. We don't want our children to feel that in order to be loved they must be something they are not. And competition over things one cannot control, like one's physical attributes, only causes anxiety.

We shouldn't fear that children will be uninterested in learning. They are born wanting to learn—our challenge is to ensure that we keep this wonderful enthusiasm alive. We can support their natural desire to do their best, whatever that means for each child.

Since children learn most from our own example, we might need to ask ourselves, "Do I show respect for my child just as he or she is? Do I show respect for myself just as I am?" If not, we can work on changing our own attitudes. We all want to be able to say, "I feel good about myself!"

Cornelia Maude Spelman, M.S.W.

I feel good about myself.

Somebody loves me just as I am.

I don't have to look like anyone else, be the same size, or do the same things.

It's fine to be me.

I am somebody's friend.

Somebody likes me just as I am.

I don't have to be first.

I don’t have to be best.
All I need to do is try my hardest.

Some things are easy for me to do;

other things are hard.
But that's OK,
because everyone is different.

When I paint or make things, they
are not like anyone else's.

Somebody likes what I paint
or make.

I am someone's helper.

I feel good when I can help.

I like making new friends,

and I like learning new things.

If I make a mistake,

I can try again.

I feel good about myself!